D0909252

CAVES!
UNDERGROUND WORLDS

Here are some other nonfiction
Redfeather Books you will enjoy

• • • • •

*Alligators: A Success Story
by Patricia Lauber

Earthworms: Underground Farmers
by Patricia Lauber

*Exploring an Ocean Tide Pool
by Jeanne Bendick

Frozen Man
by David Getz

*Great Whales: The Gentle Giants
by Patricia Lauber

In Search of the Grand Canyon
by Mary Ann Fraser

Lighthouses
by Brenda Z. Guiberson

*Salmon Story
by Brenda Z. Guiberson

*Snakes: Their Place in the Sun
by Robert M. McClung

Spotted Owl
by Brenda Z. Guiberson

*Available in paperback

·JEANNE BENDICK·

UNDERGROUND WORLDS

ILLUSTRATED BY TODD TELANDER

A REDFEATHER BOOK

HENRY HOLT AND COMPANY · NEW YORK

For Emily, who explores everything —J. B.

In memory of my grandmother,
Margaret Telander —T.T.

Henry Holt and Company, Inc./*Publishers since 1866*
115 West 18th Street/New York, New York 10011

Henry Holt is a registered trademark of Henry Holt and Company, Inc.

Published in Canada by Fitzhenry & Whiteside Ltd.,
195 Allstate Parkway, Markham, Ontario L3R 4T8.

Library of Congress Cataloging-in-Publication Data
Bendick, Jeanne. Caves!: underground worlds / Jeanne Bendick:
illustrated by Todd Telander. p. cm.—(A Redfeather Book)
1. Caves—Juvenile literature. [1. Caves.]
I. Telander, Todd, ill. II. Title. III. Series: Redfeather Books.
GB601.2.B465 1995 551.4´47—dc20 94-46519

ISBN 0-8050-2764-5/First Edition—1995

Printed in the United States of America on acid-free paper. ∞

10 9 8 7 6 5 4 3 2 1

Permission for the use of the following photographs is
gratefully acknowledged:

page 2 © Luray Caverns, Virginia; page 8 © Norbert Wu; pages 16, 30, 32, and
52 © Laurence Parent; page 24 © Carlsbad Caverns National Park; page 40
© Robert Frerck/Odyssey Productions/Chicago; pages 48 and 49 © French
Government Tourist Office; page 52 © Israel Antiquities Authority; page 59
© Library of Congress; page 60 by permission of the Houghton Library,
Harvard University.

CONTENTS

CAVES!

UNDERGROUND WORLDS

Caves are some of the most beautiful places on earth.

1

CAVES!

What are black on the inside, green or rocky outside, have chimneys and pits, huge rooms and tiny passages, weird shapes and running water, and have been around for millions of years?

Caves!

Caves are secret places. Even though people walk on top of them all the time, caves are almost always discovered by accident.

Hundreds of years ago, people searching for unicorn horns wandered into Adelsberg, the grandest cave in Europe and one of the first to be explored.

A Kentucky hunter, tracking a wounded bear, found Mammoth Cave, the longest cave system yet known.

Two shepherds in Israel, looking for a lost lamb, found a cave near the Dead Sea that was heaped with ancient scrolls containing original books of the Old Testament.

Four French boys, looking for their dog, fell into a cave where the walls were covered with wonderful pictures of animals, painted thousands of years ago. That cave is called Lascaux.

A boy and his father, who followed some mysterious, roaring smoke, discovered Carlsbad Caverns in New Mexico, one of the biggest and most beautiful caves in the world.

A scientist examining an aerial photograph of Borneo was sure there were great caverns under the landscape. He was right. The Sarawak Chamber in Borneo's Muli National Park is by far the largest known chamber in the world.

Caves!

They are on islands and under mountains and under the ocean.

They are on every continent. There are so many caves on earth that they are almost another continent underneath us.

Caves are mysterious. There have always been myths about them—legends peopled by supernatural beings.

An ancient Greek myth told that any cave might be the entrance to Hades, the underworld, which was guarded by a monstrous, many-headed dog named Cerberus.

Cerberus had a dragon's tail and snakes growing out of his back and neck. Different stories said he had three, or fifty, or even a hundred heads. Cerberus ate ghosts who tried to escape from Hades. He also threatened the dead who were coming in, but he could be bribed with honey cakes.

An ancient Japanese myth said that the world became dark in the evening when Amatseru, their sun goddess, went into her cave.

A Scandinavian folktale told of trolls who had to live in caves because they would burst if the sun shone on their faces.

An Irish folktale said that caves opened on Halloween, and monsters and demons rushed out.

An old Welsh myth says that King Arthur and his knights still sleep in a cave in Wales, waiting to be called when they are needed to fight a great battle.

If outer space is the universe around our planet earth, caves could be called "inner space," part of the world beneath us, in the earth's crust.

Caves are some of the most beautiful places on our planet.

Caves are mysteries waiting to be discovered and explored.

Caves hold secrets—secrets of animal evolution, secrets of the history of people on earth, and secrets of the history of the earth itself.

2

CAVES AND THE EARTH'S CRUST

Some caves are very, very deep, but still they are all found in the outer layer of the earth, the layer called the earth's *crust*. The crust is the part of the earth you see around you, the part you stand on.

Mountains and valleys, plains and deserts are all part of the earth's crust. Everywhere, under the oceans and under cities, under soil, sand, and rivers, the crust is made of rock.

Since the earth formed, about 4½ billion years ago, the crust has changed shape many times. Some rocks have formed and cracked, melted and cooled, been pushed up into mountains and sucked down under the crust. Continents have formed and drifted apart. Everywhere, the earth keeps changing. Usually the change is slow. Occasionally, an earthquake or a volcano makes a fast change in the crust.

Compared with the size of the earth, the crust isn't very

thick. It's only about twenty miles thick under the continents and only about four miles thick under the oceans.

Under the crust is the layer of the earth called the *mantle.*

The mantle is rock too, but it's not hard like the rock in the crust. It seems to be more like clay or thick taffy. Nobody has ever seen the mantle, but it has been explored with the instruments that detect and measure earthquakes, which start in the mantle. Scientists think the rock in the mantle flows very, very slowly. The ice in a glacier, which looks like solid ice, flows that way, too.

The mantle rock, which is called *magma,* is flaming hot. Magma boils out through the crust when a volcano explodes. In other places, steam from the magma comes out through vents in the crust. These places are called *geysers.* There are geysers in Yellowstone National Park and in the volcanic plateau of North Island, New Zealand. There are many geysers in Iceland, which is largely volcanic. Volcanoes in Iceland push up new islands.

All the rock in the crust is not the same. Some of it is formed when magma blows up through the crust or seeps through it. Rocks formed this way are called *igneous* rocks.

Under the sea, caves wind through coral.

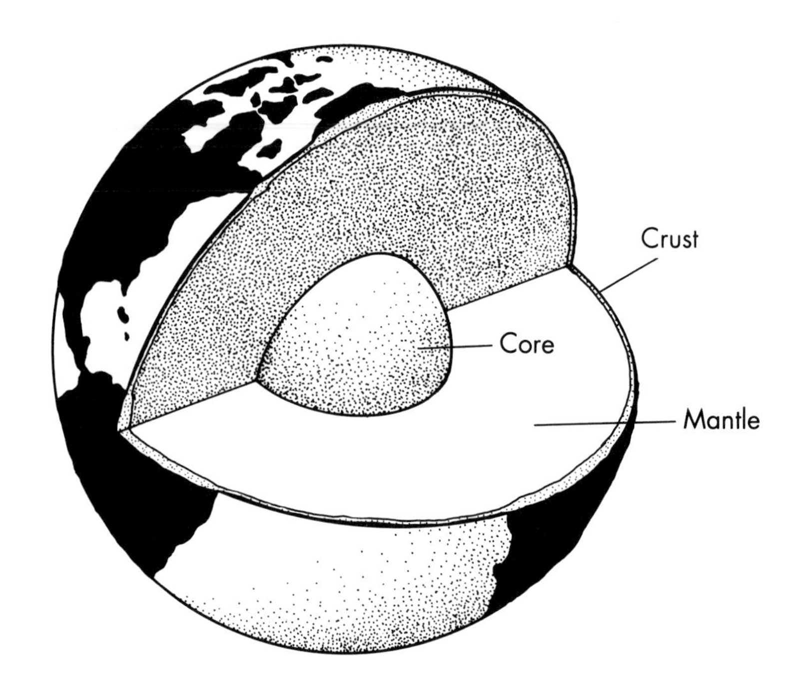

The Layers of the Earth

If you compare the earth to a peach, then the crust is no thicker than the peach skin. (An ocean would be no deeper than a pinprick in the peach skin.)

Under the earth's crust is the layer of earth called the *mantle.* The mantle would be like the part of the peach you eat.

At the center of the peach is the pit. At the center of the earth is its *core.* We don't know much about the earth's core, except that it seems to be liquid metal inside a shell of solid metal.

("Igneous" comes from an old Latin word that means "fire.")

The continents rest on igneous rocks that were formed millions of years ago. They are the *bedrock* of the earth's crust. The bedrock itself is broken into huge slabs that float on the mantle. The slabs are called *tectonic plates.*

Sedimentary rocks usually cover the bedrock, making up the top layers of the crust. They are formed when bits of sediment, which is loose stuff—minerals, sand, shells, and soil—are heaped up by wind or piled up in water and gradually squeezed together as mountains fold and wrinkle. Sedimentary rocks are usually layered. Limestone, shale, and sandstone are sedimentary rocks.

Metamorphic rocks begin as either of the other kinds. ("Metamorphic" means "changed.") They are changed deep in the crust by heat and pressure as the crust changes shape. Slate began as sedimentary shale. Marble began as sedimentary limestone. But how did limestone begin?

About 250 million years ago, even before the dinosaurs lived, the earth looked very different. The warm waters of great inland seas covered the land. Countless tiny marine animals lived in those waters. Those animals absorbed from the water a mineral called *calcite,* and used that mineral to form their shells and skeletons. Tiny, single-celled plants

How a Reef Became a Limestone Mountain

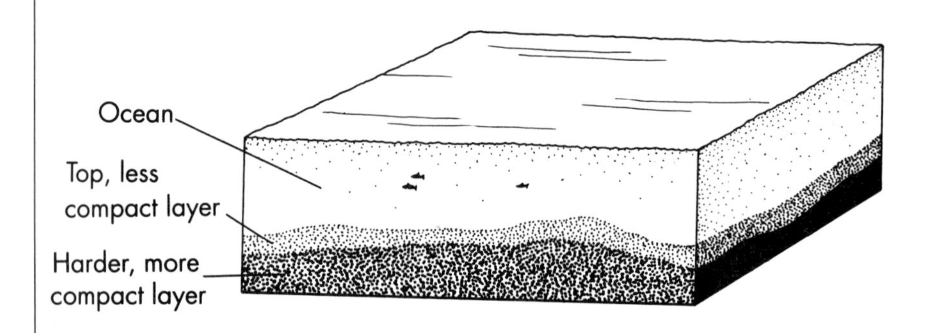

1. The skeletons of marine plants and animals began to pile up in the shallow seas. That made a reef. As the layers piled up on top they made the layers below harden and compact.

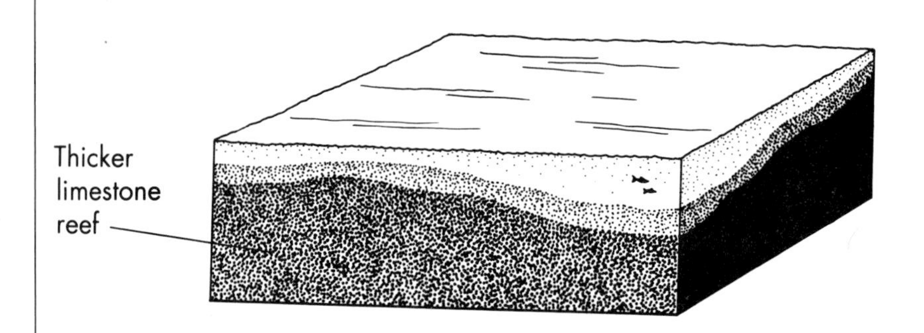

2. Over millions of years, the underwater reef grew thicker and thicker.

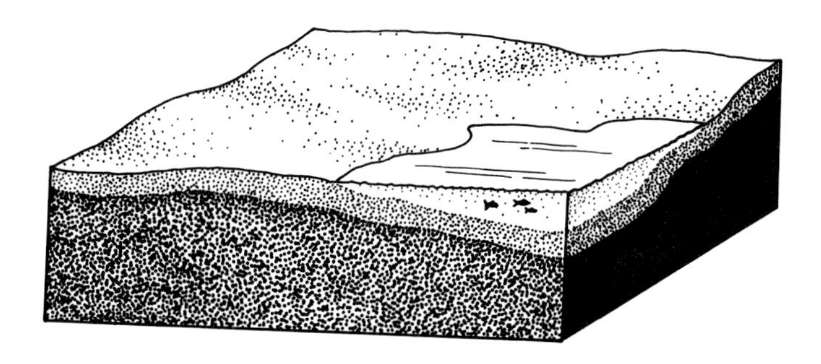

3. Seas dried up. Now the reef was sticking out of the water.

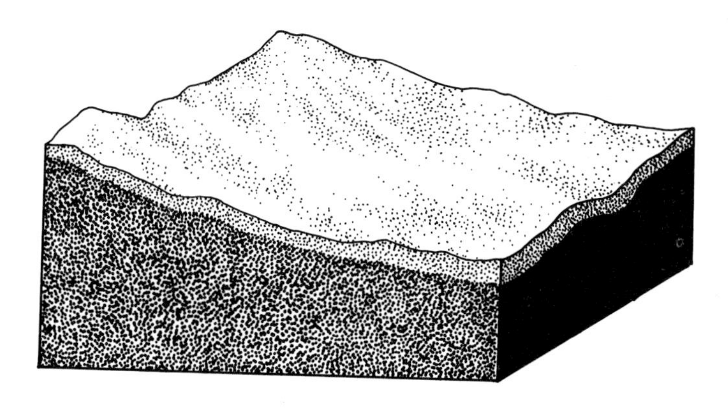

4. Earthquakes and other movements of the earth's crust shoved the reef up into mountains.

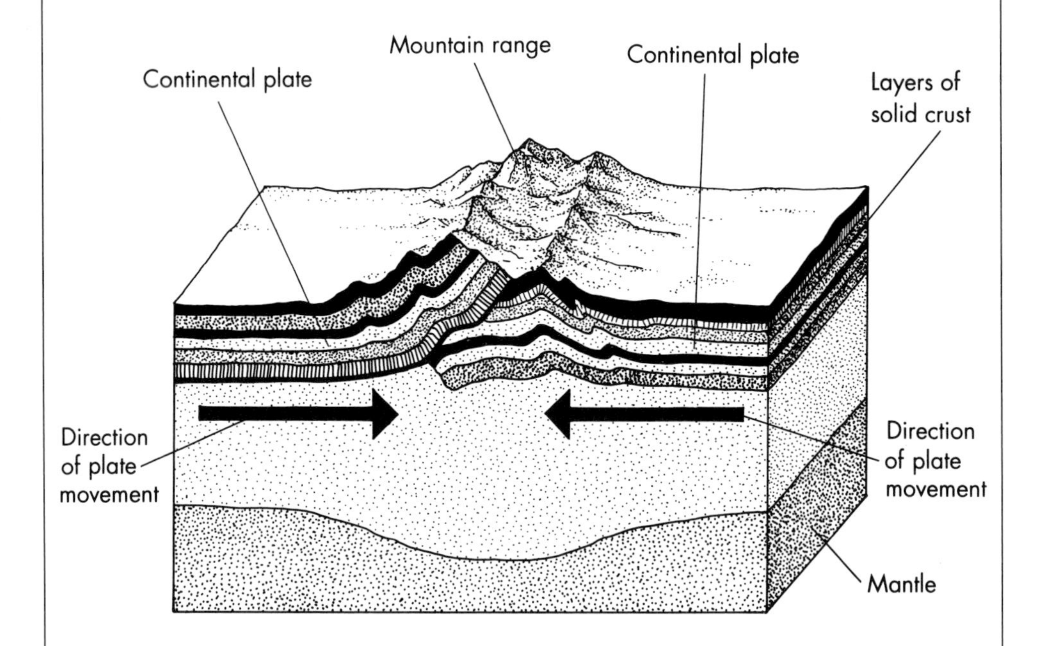

The Crust Is Like a Jigsaw Puzzle

The earth's crust is divided into sections called *tectonic plates.* The plates float on the mantle.

There are six giant plates, with some smaller ones in the big plates. Sometimes plates push against each other, shoving the crust up into mountains.

Sometimes one plate slowly sinks under the edge of another, causing the plates to slide past each other.

These movements take thousands of years.

also used calcite to make the cases that enclosed them. (The same kinds of marine plants and animals still live in our warm oceans.)

Over time, as those marine organisms lived and died, their shells and skeletons piled on top of each other and a reef began to grow. It was something like the coral reefs in the oceans today, but it grew much bigger and thicker. Layers and layers piled up, squashing the shells below them into harder and harder layers. The reef grew this way for millions of years until it was hundreds of feet thick and miles across. More minerals from the water seeped into the tiny spaces between the piled-up skeletons, cementing them together into the rock known as limestone.

Most of the earth's caves are found in sedimentary limestone.

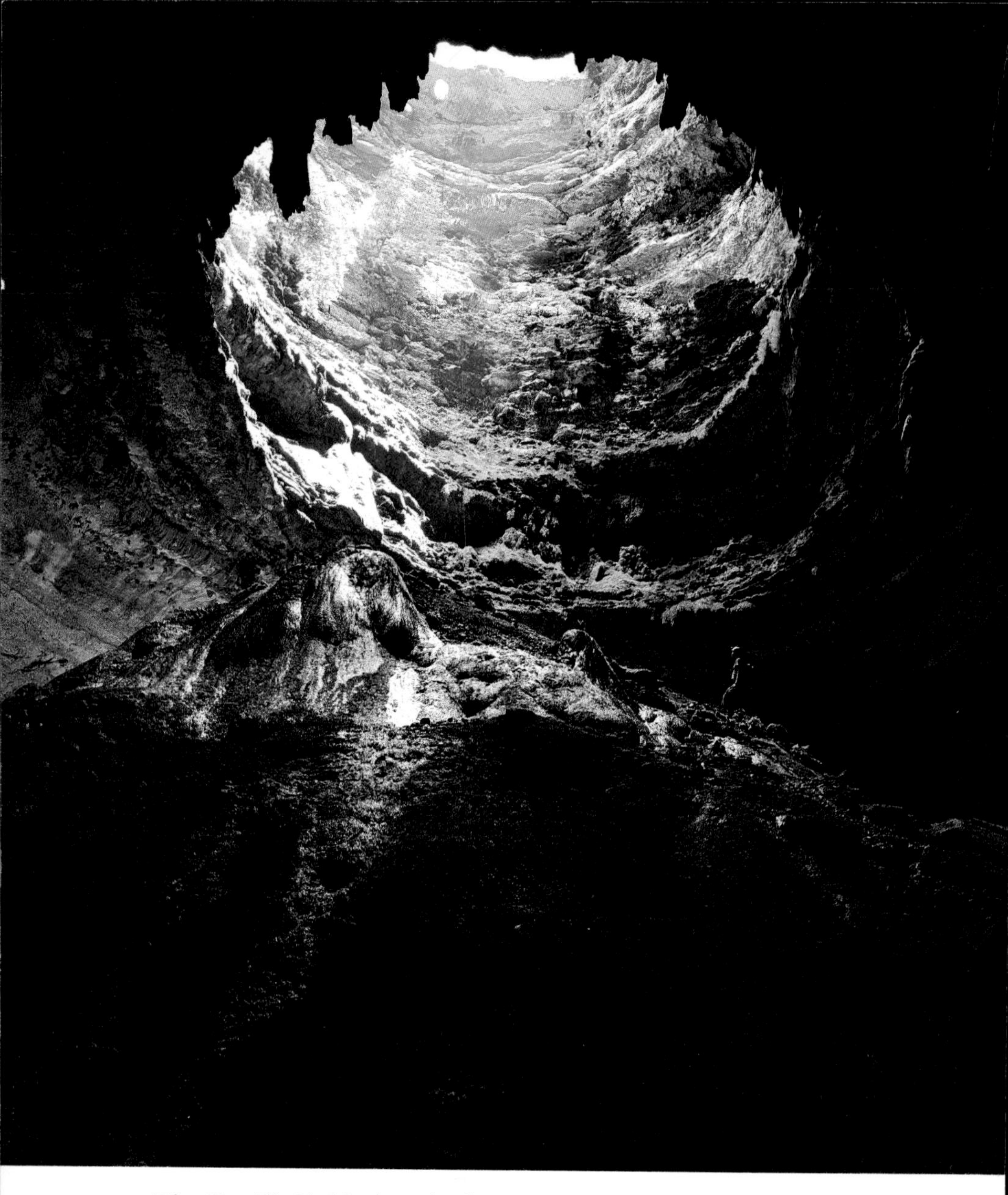

The Devil's Sinkhole, which is in Texas, is immense.

3

HOW CAVES BEGIN

Millions of years pass. More sediment—sand, soil, and other stuff—piles on top of the reef.

New currents in the water add layers of clay or different kinds of rock. The layers are called *beds.* The places where different kinds of layers meet in the limestone are called *bedding planes.*

Sometimes a change of climate makes changes in the reef. The reef might even stick up out of the water for a while and form a hard surface.

The earth's landscape keeps changing. Earthquakes shift the surface. Some of the great plates that make up the earth's crust push against each other and buckle the crust up into mountains. Sea levels fall. The reefs are pushed up into the air, up with the mountains. (Most limestone caves

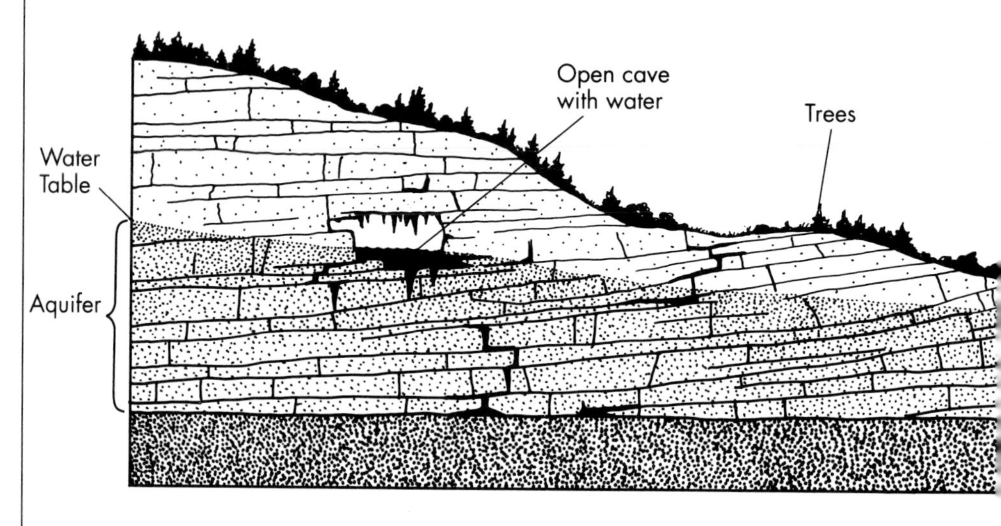

The Water Table

Almost everywhere on or under the surface of the earth there is fresh water. On the surface, the water may be a river or a lake. But even when you can't see water, somewhere underground there is a zone that is filled with water. All the cracks in the rocks are flooded. The soil has as much water as it can hold. This zone of underground water is called the *aquifer.* (When people dig wells, they are digging down into the aquifer.)

Below the aquifer, there is a bed of rock that keeps the water from

are found in mountains. Very high mountains have very deep caves.)

Trees and other plants grow on the mountains over the old reef.

Cracks develop in the limestone.

This all takes time. Time is important in cave-making.

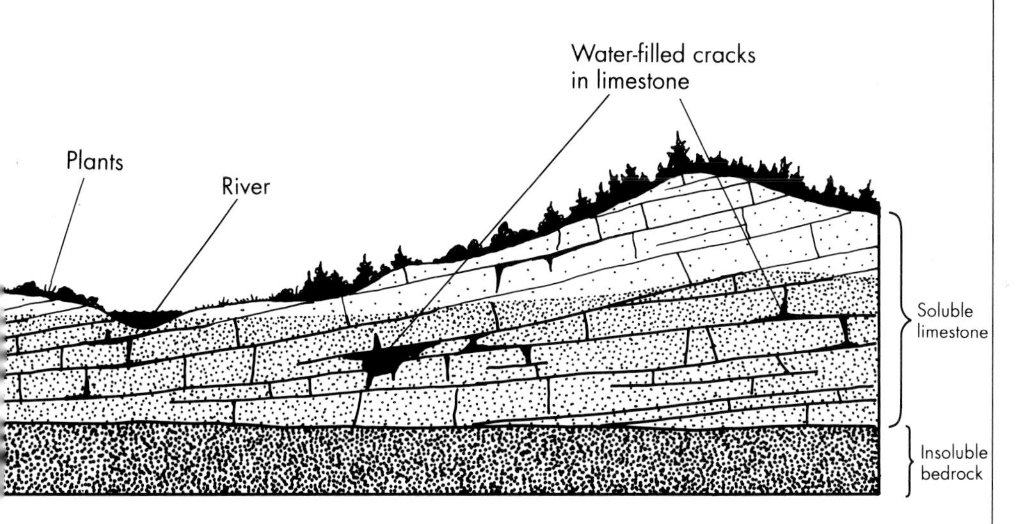

going deeper. The upper level of the aquifer is called the *water table.*

In some places, the water table is at or near the surface of the earth. In other places it is far underground. The water table can rise or fall, depending on the climate, the amount of rain, and even the amount of water used by people.

Surface water always flows down toward the level of the water table in any way it can. It digs out passages for itself, following the slope of the bedding planes and the directions of cracks or *joints* in the limestone. That's why the passages in a cave system go this way and that.

Another important ingredient is water—plenty of fresh water. Rainwater sinks into the soil, down through long-buried plants, roots, and leaves, down to the limestone and into the cracks.

On its way through the soil, the water absorbs *carbon dioxide,* a gas that plants make as they grow. The carbon dioxide mixes with the water and makes it slightly acid. That helps dissolve the calcite in the limestone.

The water seeps down and down, dissolving more limestone and carrying it along, so the cracks get bigger.

Something else helps to make a cave. Far below the soil and the cracks, a river that has gone underground is carving out a *passage* for itself. The fast-flowing water completely fills the passage, grinding away the rock to make a cave. Caves formed in water-filled passages are called *phreatic caves.*

As the water digs the passage deeper, the water level in the passage drops and there is air above the water. Still the river keeps on digging. Caves formed by running water with air above it are called *vadose caves.*

Limestone cave systems are usually a combination of both kinds. The upper, older passages are vadose caves. They may even be dry. The deeper, water-filled passages are phreatic.

As a cave gets bigger and dryer, the rocks may shift and move. Sometimes rocks in the cave roof fall away. When many big rocks fall out of the cave ceiling, huge rooms called *chambers* can open up. The Big Room in Carlsbad Caverns, New Mexico, is a third of a mile wide and higher than a twenty-five-story building. Very big caves with chambers and many passages are *caverns* or *cave systems.*

Karst

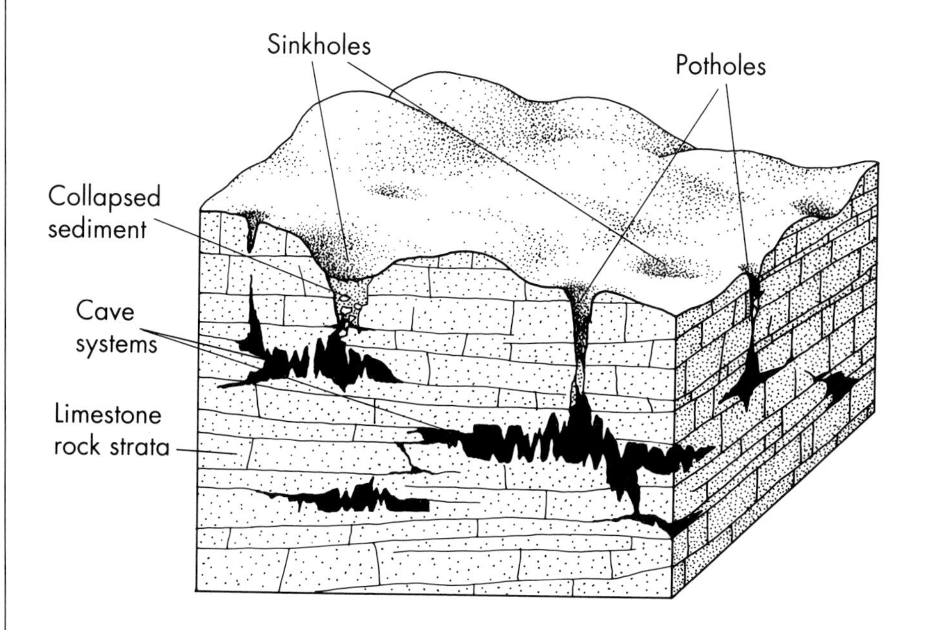

Because a karst area has such a special, bumpy shape, a scientist who was examining an aerial photograph of the Borneo jungle decided that there must be caves under some odd-looking hills. Sure enough, an expedition found a huge cave system there, in the Muli National Park. The Sarawak Chamber in those caves is the largest known chamber in the world. The next two largest chambers—the Big Room in Carlsbad Caverns, New Mexico, and Salle de la Verna in Pierre St. Martin's cave in France—would fit together in the Sarawak Chamber with room to spare.

Nobody is quite sure why in some places there are huge chambers but the passages leading in and out of them are narrow, twisting in different directions. Cave explorers can get lost in them. In most cave systems, the big rooms aren't connected to each other, or the passages connecting them are so small that crawling is the only way to get through them. Then suddenly—a great, domed chamber.

The earth's surface is constantly changing. Water, wind, and ice grind away rocks and move soil, sand, and pebbles. These changes that wear away the surface are called *erosion.* Plants, people, and other living things change the surface in their own ways.

Areas of the earth where the limestone is deeply dissolved and eroded are called *karst* regions.

Long ago, the ancient Celts called the bare, bumpy, deeply cracked and holey limestone area between the Alps and the Adriatic Sea "the Karst." (There are over ten thousand caves there.) When the Romans came they used that name, too. Now, anywhere on earth, formations like that are called karst.

Karst is like a sponge. Rivers on the surface may suddenly vanish into the ground of a karst region. There are big, oddly-shaped cracks and much bigger openings called *potholes* and *sinkholes.*

Potholes are narrow holes, hundreds of feet deep. Sinkholes aren't as deep but they may be wider than ten city blocks.

Potholes and sinkholes can be the entrances to caves. Sinkholes are also called *dolines.*

Most of the caves on earth are found in karst regions. Some scientists say that karst may cover up to 10 percent of the earth's crust.

A soda straw is a beginning stalactite. It is *much* smaller than this.

4

CAVE DECORATIONS—
DRAPERIES AND SODA STRAWS, FLOWERS AND PEARLS

Even after those first millions of years, a cave doesn't look like much—just some big rock rooms connected by little passages. In some places, there are deep *shafts* going down to other levels, and in other places there are bridges where rock has fallen away. There may be pools or lakes and somewhere there's a river. Everything is bare and dark. The only sound is of water—water rushing far below and water dripping from the ceiling, down the walls, across the floor.

Slowly, dripping water will make the cave beautiful, starting from the top. Water seeping through cracks in the ceiling dissolves the limestone and leaves a drop of calcite on the ceiling. Drop by drop, over hundreds and thousands of years, the calcite icicle on the ceiling grows—maybe an inch a year, maybe an inch every hundred years, sometimes only an inch every thousand years.

These limestone icicles are called *stalactites.*

How fast a stalactite grows depends on what the ground is like on the surface over the cave. If the surface is covered by forest the stalactite grows faster than if the surface is grass. That's because of the carbon dioxide plants release during *photosynthesis.* When carbon dioxide mixes with rainwater, it becomes *carbonic acid,* which dissolves limestone much faster than rainwater alone does. Bigger plants, such as trees, make more carbon dioxide than grass does. If the surface is bare rock, the stalactite grows even more slowly.

Often the drip from the end of the stalactite splashes onto the cave floor underneath it and another kind of formation grows there. This is called a *stalagmite.*

Some stalagmites are as skinny as the stalactites above them. They are called *totem poles.* But some are huge—in a big cavern, they may be taller than a skyscraper and bigger around than a giant redwood tree. When stalactites and stalagmites meet and join they are called *columns.* It could take 100,000 years to make a column. Columns get bigger as water drips down their sides.

Sometimes stalactites begin as *soda straws.* Soda straws

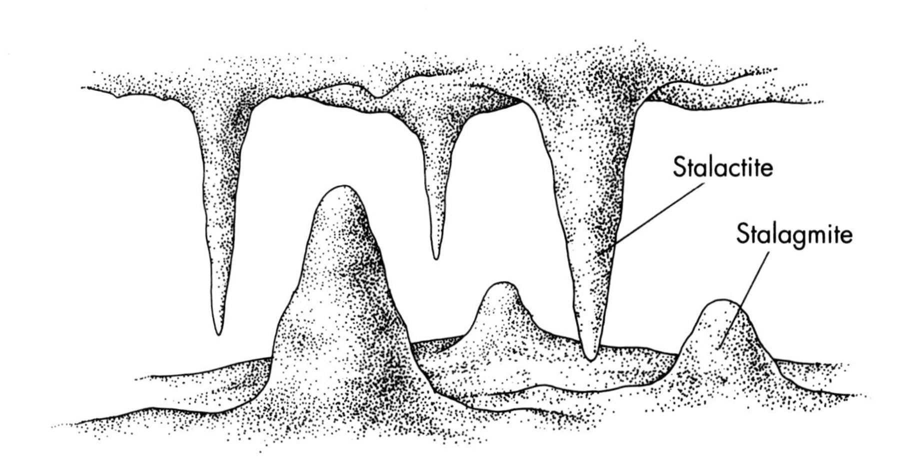

How to remember which is which: A stala**C**tite hangs from the **C**eiling. A stala**G**mite grows from the **G**round.

Two hundred years ago, in the eighteenth century, Joseph Tournefort, a French botanist (a scientist who studies plants) insisted that dripping water could never make such formations. He said that stalactites and stalagmites were plants and that they grew from seeds.

are hollow inside and the water drips through them. When the insides clog up with calcite, they are on their way to becoming stalactites. (In a few thousand years, that is.)

Nobody is quite sure how the decorations called *helictites* form. Helictites are like soda straws, but they curl and twist in every direction, even up against gravity. Maybe air currents or changes in temperature make them grow that way.

Other decorations are made of a very soft calcite called *gypsum*. As new crystals form in the cracks, the gypsum is squeezed out into the cave the way toothpaste is squeezed out of a tube. Sometimes the gypsum forms into shapes that look like flowers or butterflies. Sometimes gypsum covers a ceiling with shining needles.

Water in a cave doesn't always drip. It might seep along a slanted ceiling to form thin *draperies* that seem to hang in folds. If there has been a constant wind in the cave, the draperies don't hang straight down; they look as if they are blowing in the wind.

If some water carries white calcite and some carries red iron, the draperies may look like strips of bacon.

What goes with bacon? *Fried eggs,* of course. These formations grow in the dish-shaped tops of broken stalagmites. The whites are calcite. Other minerals color the yolks. The minerals in a cave are of many colors. You can see those colors if somebody shines an ultraviolet or infrared light on the cave walls.

Clusters of calcite balls that build up on the walls of a flooded cave are called *sea grapes* or *popcorn*.

Water seeping down the walls, over rocks, and onto the floor forms a kind of stone waterfall called *flowstone.*

A pool in the cave might make its own decorations.

helictite
soda straw
stalactite
drapery
flowstone
shelfstone
column
popcorn
cave raft
stalagmite
cave pearls

The "Klansman" stalagmite in Carlsbad Caverns National Park, New Mexico, is draped in a sheet of sinter. Formations take many kinds of fantastic shapes.

Maybe a flat shelf of stone will form around the edges or around a stalagmite in the pool. Even if the pool dries up, the *shelfstone* stays.

Can you imagine pancakes floating in a pool? These light, thin calcite formations are called *cave rafts.* If the water is disturbed, they sink.

Once in a while, a pool may have *cave pearls* in it. These form around grains of sand, adding layers of calcite in the same way that oysters form pearls. Water dripping into the pool keeps the pearls moving and rounds them out. Some cave pearls are as big as Ping-Pong balls.

Sinter is a name for all calcite cave formations.

As long as water keeps dripping into a cave and as long as shapes keep forming and growing, the cave is called a *live cave.* When the cave is dry and no water comes in, it's called a *dead cave.*

Some caves sound alive—as if they are breathing. Caves blow air out or suck it in to equalize the air pressure underground with that outside. Winds blow out of the cave when the air pressure drops and a storm is coming. Winds blow into the cave when the weather outside is fair and the air pressure there rises. Depending on where they are, some caves are windy all the time. Wind blowing through a cave helps to shape the decorations.

Cave decorations are very fragile. Even giant columns and massive stalagmites are easily broken. Touching the end of a stalactite can break off hundreds of years of its life. Early cave visitors did a lot of damage with their sooty torches, heavy boots, and graffiti, and their desire for souvenirs. You can still see the damage in almost any *show cave.* Modern visitors know better.

Salamanders in the dark zone have no eyes.

5

LIFE IN CAVES

If you step into a cave with a very large entrance, what's inside the cave may not be too different from what's just outside. There is plenty of light. Maybe there's a breeze blowing in. Ferns, mosses, and other plants are growing on the cave floor.

Birds fly in and out. Some have their nests on ledges up on the cave walls. Flies buzz. Mosquitoes hum. Crickets jump. Mice could live in the corners. If you stand very still you might see a snake.

Animals come and go in the *entrance zone.* Some spend their days or nights in the cave and the rest of the time outside. Some spend whole seasons inside. Spiders and daddy longlegs come in and stay for the winter. So do snakes. In the winter, a cave is warmer than the world outside and it is protected from snow and sleet.

Bears hibernate in caves. They half-sleep through the

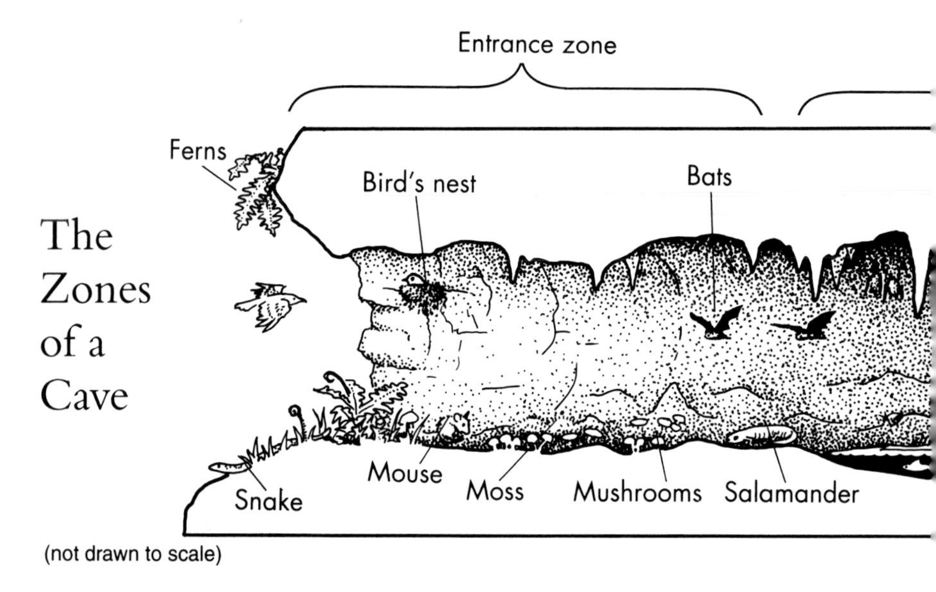

winter, maybe going out occasionally for something to eat. Mother bears give birth to their cubs there. Some bears live in caves all year round. Fifty thousand bear skeletons have been found in a cave in Austria called Dragon's Cave. Maybe the people who first found those skeletons thought they were dragons' bones. Bears used that cave for thousands of years.

Bears, porcupines, hyenas, and different kinds of great cats live part of their lives in caves.

These in-and-out animals are called *trogloxenes,* which means "cave visitors."

As you walk back into the cave, the light gets dimmer, even though you can still see the entrance. Now you are in the *twilight zone* and the animals that live here are called

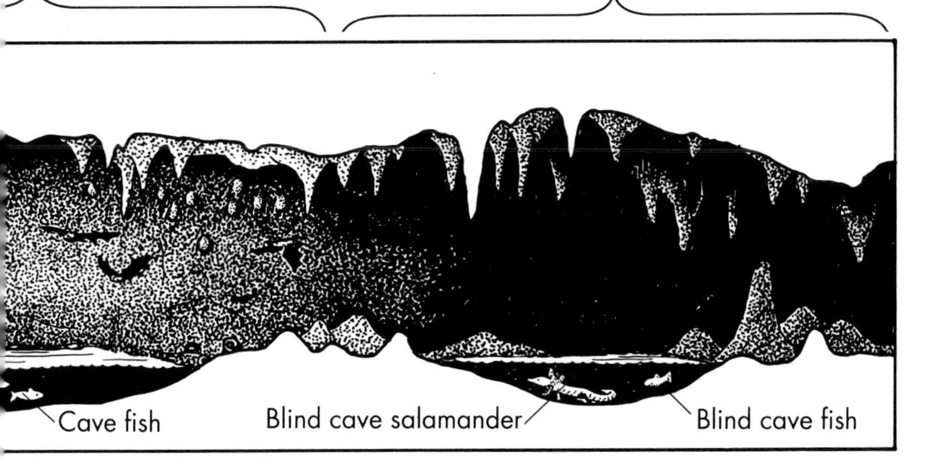

troglophiles—animals that like living in caves. The temperature in the twilight zone changes with the seasons.

Troglophiles sleep in caves during the day and go outside at night, looking for food. Owls live in the twilight zone. So do spiders, cockroaches, millipedes, salamanders, snails, and cave crickets. Many of these animals are scavengers. They are the clean-up squad, eating whatever dies in the cave. Most cave-dwelling animals live in the twilight zone.

Bats are the most important troglophiles.

In 1885, a boy and his father, who were looking for a stray cow in the New Mexico desert, traced the source of a huge, black cloud that looked like smoke but sounded like a whirlwind. The cloud was coming out of a hole in the ground. The hole was the entrance to a cave system that is now called Carlsbad Caverns, and the smoke was a cloud of a million bats that fly out of the caverns every evening in search of food.

Each bat weighs only half an ounce, but every night each one eats half its weight in insects. So together, they eat about eight tons of insects every night.

All those bats fly around in the dark without bumping into walls or into each other. Like all living things, bats are adapted to the way they live. Their claws are adapted to hanging upside down while they sleep. (In the daytime, the cave ceiling looks like a furry rug.) Their wings are adapted to fast maneuvering in flight. Their ears are very big for hearing the signals around them.

When it's flying, each bat sends out a series of very fast clicks which bounce off solid objects and return to the bat, telling it what's in front of it and how far away it is. (Sonar in a submarine works like that. Sonar bounces signals off the walls of deep sea canyons, or ships, or other submarines.)

Each bat has its own pattern of clicks so it doesn't get confused, even in the crowded bat cloud. The bats' system is called *echolocation*. They use echolocation in the dark to avoid cave walls and other bats. They use it to find the in-

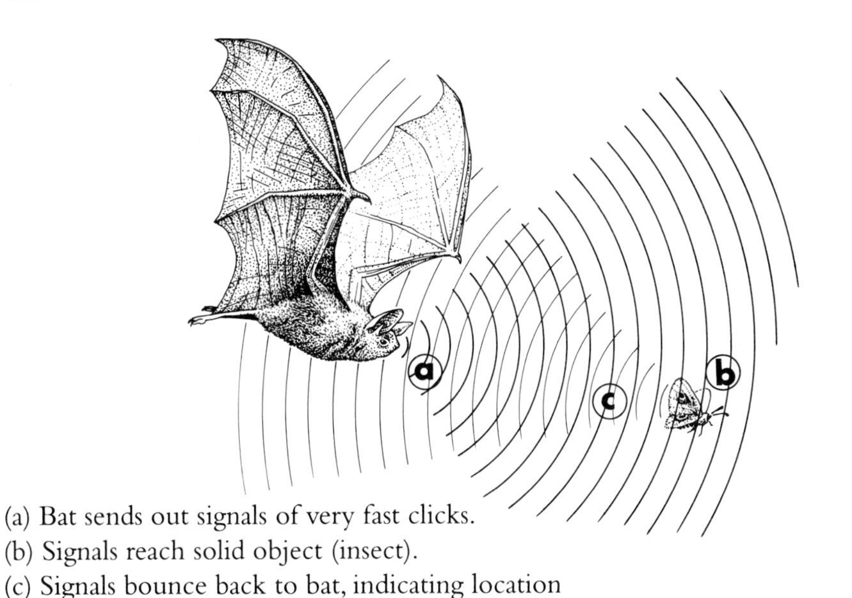

(a) Bat sends out signals of very fast clicks.
(b) Signals reach solid object (insect).
(c) Signals bounce back to bat, indicating location and distance of object.

sects that are their food. Echolocation works perfectly, even on mosquitoes.

Farther back in the cave, there is no light at all. This is called the *dark zone.* If the passage into the cave takes a sharp turn near the entrance, there may not be a twilight zone—just an entrance zone and a dark zone. If you have never been in a cave, the dark zone is darker than you can imagine. It's so dark you can almost hear the darkness.

The temperature in the dark zone doesn't change. The animals that live there are called *troglobites,* true cave dwellers. They never go outside. They cannot live anywhere else. There are tiny crustaceans, related to shrimps and lobsters. Other crustaceans, called isopods, are like bugs. There are worms, fish, salamanders, and insects. There are hundreds of kinds of troglobite beetles.

Troglobites have the same needs as animals anywhere else in the world. They need air, water, food, and a safe place to live.

Troglobites are all small. Small animals don't need much food, and troglobites have to depend on what little comes to them from outside. Some can live for months or even years without eating.

In every zone of the cave, the food chain starts outside. The animals that come and go bring food into the cave. Underground streams or heavy rains also bring in food from outside. Dead insects and other animals wash in and so does bat *guano,* or droppings. Bigger troglobites eat the smaller ones.

Most troglobites are blind; they have no eyes at all. Eyes are not useful when it's always totally dark. But their other senses—hearing, tasting, smelling, and touching—are very sharp. Most have long feelers for finding their way in the dark. They have no color. The skins of some are so thin you can see through them. They don't need protection from the sun.

Troglobites can live only in wet caves. Some, even though they have lungs and gills, take in oxygen through their skins directly from the wet air or from water flowing through the cave.

In a part of Adelsberg, there is a foot-long blind salamander called a *Proteus.* Once people believed these were baby dragons and they watched nervously for the big ones.

Troglobites seem weird, but there are no new kinds of animals among them. They are all related to similar animals in the world outside. Over a long, long time they have become adapted to the life they live in the dark.

In a cave in New Zealand, troglobite glowworms make their own light, the kind we call luminescence.

Not many kinds of animals *are* adapted to living in dark caves. There are about a million and a half kinds of invertebrates—animals without backbones. Only about 150 kinds live in dark caves. There are about half a million kinds of vertebrates—animals with backbones. Only a few blind fishes and salamanders live deep inside caves.

All big cave systems have dark zones. If artificial lighting is installed in a dark zone the lights are kept on only while visitors are there. Even so, the environment of the troglobites has been changed. Any environment is a delicate balance. People make changes that disturb that balance.

6

PEOPLE IN CAVES

People aren't troglobites, but once they were trog-loxenes. Before they learned to build houses—or anything else—they lived in caves. That was long before people kept records, in the times we call prehistoric. Even some of the prehuman creatures known as *hominids,* which means "manlike," lived in caves a million years ago. Their bones have been found in limestone caves in Africa and in China.

Modern humans are called *Homo sapiens,* which means "man the wise." There may have been several kinds of *Homo sapiens,* but the earliest we know for sure were the Neanderthals, whose remains were first found in the Neander region of Germany. Neanderthals were short and heavy

In Cappadocia, Turkey, some people live in caves cut into volcanic tuff.

with skulls shaped differently from ours, but they had big brains. About thirty thousand years ago, they were replaced by the Cro-Magnons, who looked the way we do now.

Caves were used for dwellings about a million years ago, even before the last period of the Ice Age. (During the Ice Age, there were four periods when ice covered much of the northern half of the earth, with three warmer periods in between.) Some of the same caves were used over and over, for thousands of years. Over time, groups of people moved in and out.

When a cave was abandoned, leaves, soil, and sand blew into the cave, gradually covering the litter and leavings of the group and making a new "floor." When a later group moved onto that floor, the same thing happened. Each group left its own kind of cave litter—tools, bits of clothing, the bones of the animals they ate, even the bones of the people themselves. Scientists learn a lot about how humans lived over thousands of years by studying what they left behind. Even ashes and charred wood tell a story.

Archaeologists have found caves with seven or eight layers. Each layer was the home of a different group at a later time. Sometimes there were long periods between layers. Each layer tells us more about the history of those cave dwellers.

Caves were a natural place for early people to live. They provided shelter from the weather and the climate, especially during the cold years of the Ice Age. Just inside the cave entrance, there might be a windbreak made of branches and animal skins. Many families would live together in the entrance zone of a big cave.

It was safer to live in a cave than outside. The cave walls provided protection on three sides, and usually there was a hearth made of loose stones just outside the entrance. A fire there frightened away wolves, cave bears, cave lions, and other dangerous animals. Fires also kept people warm and were the only way they had of cooking the meat that was a big part of their diet. Cooked meat was not as tough as raw meat, and it tasted better.

There are places in the world where people still live in caves. In Turkey, near a place called Kayseri Cappadocia, volcanic action thousands of years ago left queer-looking towers of a volcanic material called tuff. The towers look like fat, upside-down ice-cream cones. People have dug caves in them and they have been homes for two thousand years. Now the caves even have electric lights.

In China, caves have been cut into a porous rock called loess. There are so many people in China that there aren't enough houses, so thousands of people live in those caves.

Early Cave Dwellers

The earliest cave dwellers we know about were the not-quite-humans called *Homo erectus.* They lived from about 1 million to 500,000 years ago. *Homo erectus* made crude tools—first from pebbles, later by chipping stone. Charred rocks and ashes show that they used fire.

They like them. The temperature is comfortable and they don't have to pay rent. If a family needs another room, they just dig it.

Ancient cave people had hard lives. It wasn't easy to stay safe, stay warm, and find enough food. You would think that day-to-day living took up all their energy. But early humans found time to do other things, too. Some of them used the deepest, darkest, far-inside caves for something else.

The Neanderthals lived from about 70,000 to about 35,000 years ago. They used stones, bone, and wood for tools and weapons, and they made clothes out of animal skins. We can tell, from excavations in or near their caves, that they buried their dead.

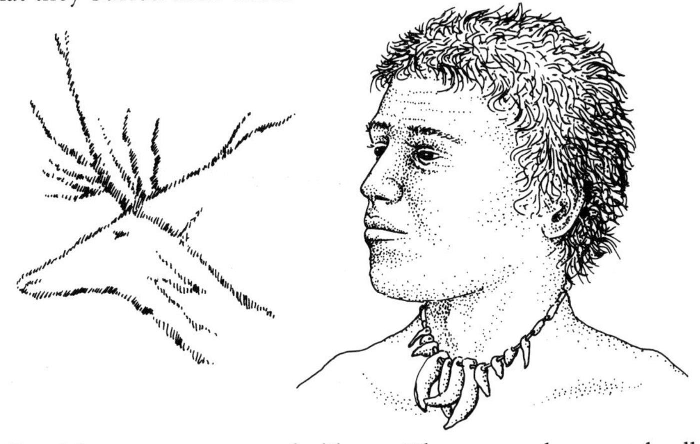

The Cro-Magnons were people like us. They were the cave dwellers who painted their cave walls and carved statues. When they learned to heat metals they made even better tools and weapons. By the time they were smelting copper, bronze, and iron they were also building shelters for themselves. Caves were no longer their homes.

They painted.

The first paintings were discovered in 1879 when Don Marcellino de Sautuola, an archaeologist, was working in a cave on his land in Altamira, in northern Spain. His small daughter was with him and she was bored. Holding her candle, she wandered back through a passage into another cave. Suddenly she shouted, again and again, for her father. He came running with his larger torch, which he aimed at the roof of the cave, where she was pointing. Animals! Huge animals, painted on the ceiling and the walls in shades of red and purple, outlined in black. There were deer, wild boar, horses, and bison—the same animals whose ancient bones have been found in caves.

Professor Juan Vilanova, a Madrid geologist, estimated that the paintings were many thousands of years old. Nobody believed it. They said the paintings were so beautiful that they must be modern fakes. Surely, ignorant cave people of long ago could not have made them!

Both Don Marcellino and Vilanova had been dead for years before more cave art was discovered. There were other painted caves in Spain. Some had paintings and sculptures. Engravings were scratched into the walls.

There are beautiful paintings in French caves, too.

The cave paintings in Spain and France were made during the Paleolithic period, or Old Stone Age. Scientists think most cave paintings were done between 18,000 and 11,000 years ago. Their colors were not vegetable dyes—those would have faded long ago. Instead the artists used earth minerals from the caves. They used iron oxides and manganese to make red, gray, brown, and purple. Their white was calcite, and they made black by burning wood into charcoal.

The artists ground their colors into powders, which they kept in tubes made of hollowed-out bones. When they began painting, the artists mixed their colors with water or with minerals such as talc, feldspar, and mica. They mixed their colors in hollow rocks, or barnacle shells, or even in skulls.

They painted with brushes, with fur pads, and with their fingers. They blew paint through hollow reeds. They drew animals first with charcoal, then they painted the colors. Everywhere in the caves they stenciled their own hands by taking a mouthful of paint, putting their hands on the walls, and blowing the paint around them. (All over the world, ancient cave artists have done the same thing.)

We know how they worked because those artists left their tools behind. They left flint blades for carving on walls and scrapers for mixing and smearing. They built scaffolds to reach high on walls and ceilings. They needed

What Happened at Lascaux

After the famous paintings were discovered in the darkness of the Lascaux cave in France, fifteen hundred people a day came to the cave to see the paintings. Then something terrible began to happen.

Small, green spots appeared on the walls. Colonies of bacteria and algae grew on the paintings. The colors started to run. So many people, simply by breathing, polluted the air in the cave. Their breaths condensed on the cool walls and wet the paintings.

Something else was happening. Electric lights had been installed so visitors could see the paintings better. The lights made ferns, mosses, and lichens grow. The whole environment of the cave was changing and the paintings couldn't survive in it.

In 1961, the French government closed the cave to visitors. Scientists worked frantically to find a "cure" for the sick cave before all the paintings were destroyed. And they found it. The paintings were sprayed with antibiotics, followed by a bath of formaldehyde and detergent. All the algae disappeared, and the paintings are now as beautiful as they were when they were first discovered.

The cave, called Lascaux I, is still closed, except to scientists.

But Lascaux II has been created. The paintings there were reproduced by artists who used the same materials and methods that the original artists used. Lascaux II is open to visitors. The same thing has happened to the Altamira Cave in Spain.

light for working in those dark zones, so they burned charcoal, pine torches, and animal fat in hollow stones. The smoke from the torches blackened the ceilings above the paintings.

Scientists aren't sure why the artists painted in those dark, secret places deep in their caves, but they think the artists were painting the animals they hoped the hunters would kill. Or maybe they were paying respect to the brave animals they admired.

All the cave artists didn't live in Europe. African paintings in the rock caves at Tassili, Algeria, in the Sahara, showed life as it was thousands of years ago, before the area became a desert. Tassili artists drew horses, cattle, giraffes, camels, and buffalo. European cave artists didn't paint people but the Tassili artists did. They painted real-looking people going about their daily lives. They also made a kind of writing that is different from any kind archaeologists know. So far, nobody has figured out what the Tassili writing means.

There are ancient Inca paintings in caves high in the Andes Mountains and other prehistoric rock art across North and South America. Many of these paintings show animals and the people who hunted them.

Some North American Indians used their painted caves

for special purposes—for initiations into the tribe, for healing the sick, and as "dreaming places." We know about those things because legends and customs have been passed down through many generations. They still exist today.

Nobody knows how many art caves there are, still hidden. But we're sure they're there, and when they're found there will be new puzzles and new answers.

In 1991, a group of scuba divers swam into a cave entrance 121 feet below the surface of the Mediterranean Sea at Cap Morgiou, near Marseilles, in France. They swam through a very long passage which led slowly upward until they found themselves in a huge cave. Part of the cave was flooded, part was above the water. Everywhere on the walls were charcoal drawings. There were many hand prints. There were deer and bison, some kind of great cat, and seals and penguins.

Penguins! Did penguins ever live in the Mediterranean Sea? Scientists say the drawings were made about 18,000 years ago, during the last period of the Ice Age. Penguins could have lived there then. How else could the artists have drawn them? During that time, all of the cave was on dry land. There was probably an easier entrance somewhere above it, but so far that entrance hasn't been uncovered.

The Dead Sea Scrolls

In 1947, two shepherds looking for a lost sheep wandered into a cave in the cliffs that border the Dead Sea. In a dark corner, they found a heap of crumbling parchment and leather scrolls. The scrolls were written more than two thousand years ago, in ancient Hebrew and Aramaic. They contain books of the Old Testament and they also tell of events in that time. Since their discovery, scholars have been piecing the scrolls together, translating them, and working to preserve them. If it hadn't been for those dark, dry caves in which they were hidden, the scrolls would have been lost forever.

Painted caves are in secret places, usually discovered by accident. As others are found, we will learn new things about the cave people who painted them.

Some caves are beautiful; some are very useful. Because the temperature and humidity are constant deep inside caves, they are good places for storing things.

Today, wines are stored in caves, for aging.
Cheeses ripen in caves.
Oil reserves are stored in some caves.
Precious documents are safe in secret caves.

Underground passages are like wormholes through a cave.

7

BRAVE CAVE EXPLORERS

There are thousands and thousands of caves around the world. Many haven't been discovered yet. Most of the others have been explored only by *cavers* (or *spelunkers* or *potholers*)—brave, adventurous amateurs whose hobby is exploring caves, and by *speleologists,* scientists who study caves.

Caves in their natural state, with all or parts of them unexplored, are called *wild caves.*

Over years or centuries, some spectacular caves have been prepared so that ordinary visitors with no caving experience can enjoy the fantastic shapes, the wonderful colors, the mystery and excitement of the world under the everyday world. These caves are called show caves.

If the entrance to the cave is a deep *shaft,* there are stairs going down, with a hand rail to hold on to. If the cave is very deep, there's an elevator to take visitors down and bring them back to the surface. Paths through passages and caverns are fairly smooth and very well lit, with railings at the edges where paths are along chasms. Dramatic lighting shows off strange shapes and the ceiling formations, no matter how high they are.

There are bridges over ravines and rivers, boats for riding down rivers and across lakes. There may even be railway cars to carry passengers deep into the caverns. If you have to squeeze through a narrow passage there won't be an unpleasant surprise at the other end. Millions of people enjoy visiting show caves.

It isn't like that for the explorers of wild caves. An unexplored cave can be very dangerous.

Nobody knows how big an unexplored cave is, or where the passages lead.

You might walk and crawl through miles of passages and come to a dead end.

You could get stuck in a narrow passage.

You might step under a freezing waterfall or fall into a river.

There could be deep shafts in your way or mountains of boulders choking the passage.

You could get completely lost.

Even today, with good lights and specially designed equipment, cavers need to be experienced and careful when they explore wild caves.

After ancient people stopped living in the entrance zones of caves in Europe, very few people ventured into them. Some thought caves were entrances to Hell. Others were sure that dragons and monsters lived there, lying in wait for anyone who dared to come in.

The ancient Native Americans weren't afraid of caves. More than two thousand years ago, they were mining caves for gypsum and crystals. Two days' journey into Mammoth Cave, in Kentucky, explorers found reed torches and primitive mining tools. Even farther into Mammoth, they found the mummified body of someone who had died there 2,300 years ago.

Slowly, over the years, more daring and curious people began exploring the caves near where they lived. Visitors came into Adelsberg in the thirteenth century. We know because they scratched their names and some dates on the wall near the entrance.

About four hundred years ago, fortune seekers ventured into several German caves looking for treasure. The treasure was unicorn horns, which were valuable because they were supposed to cure many kinds of ills. Nobody had ever seen a unicorn—they were thought to be extinct—but maybe they had lived in caves, so the horns would still be there. Other animals *had* lived in the caves during past ages and the searchers brought out any old bones that looked like horns, ground them up, and sold them as medicine.

More than three hundred years ago, in the 1670s and '80s, Baron Johann Valvasor, a travel writer of the time, visited dozens of caves in the karst area of Europe. He wrote imaginative reports, made sketches of monstrous creatures turned to stone, and drew elaborate maps.

He described bottomless pits, enormous halls, and fantastic formations. He published four books describing his adventures and observations. The baron was a great exaggerator, but he was the first person to make any kind of scientific investigation of caves.

In 1747, Emperor Francis I of the Holy Roman Empire, which at that time included Germany, Austria, Hungary, former Yugoslavia, Belgium, the Netherlands, part of France, and a lot of Italy, ordered a court scientist, Joseph Nagel, to explore the caves of his empire. Nagel started at Adelsberg because the entrance zone was familiar. He took with him an Italian artist, Carlo Beduzzi. (In those days, an artist did what a photographer does on modern expeditions.)

Baron Valvasor's drawings were more imaginative than accurate.

There were only torches and candles for light, and certainly those weren't bright enough for anyone to see the size of a cavern. Nagel had an inventive idea. He fastened torches to wooden boards and tied the boards to geese. When members of the expedition threw stones at the geese, the frightened birds flew up and out into the cavern, lighting it with the torches. The emperor must have been

Stephen Bishop and Mammoth Cave

Stephen Bishop was a young slave who explored Mammoth Cave all by himself with just a lantern and a rope. Over the years, he visited unexplored caverns, crossed deep chasms, and discovered underground rivers. He taught himself to read so he could read technical books about caves.

In 1842, he drew a freehand map of the cave, showing hundreds of rooms, passages, and rivers. His map was so accurate that it was used for many years.

happy with Nagel's work, because he made him the court mathematician.

About a hundred years later, Professor Adolf Schmidl of the Vienna Academy of Science explored Adelsberg in a more scientific way. He and his son built a tiny wooden canoe for paddling down the Pivka River, which runs through the cave. They could even take the canoe apart, so each could drag a piece of canoe where the river was too shallow to float it. They carried candles and oil lamps to light their way.

Sometimes the water level in the river was low. But occasionally, there were big thunderstorms outside, which flooded water into the cave. Once, Schmidl and his son were in the cave when the river rose so high that it filled the low-ceilinged passages between the explorers and the cave entrance, a quarter of a mile away. To conserve their light, the explorers put out their candles and sat in their canoe for hours, in the cold darkness, wondering how long it would be before the water went down again and they could paddle out in safety.

In the 1880s, a French lawyer, Edouard-Alfred Martel, became the father of modern *speleology*—the science of cave exploration. Martel visited his first cave when he was seven years old and cave exploring became the most important thing in his life. He had promised his father that he would become a lawyer, and he did, but he spent all his vacations exploring caves.

At first, Martel went into caves wearing a starched, high-collared shirt, a frock coat and striped trousers, and a derby hat with a candle strapped to the front. Later, he began inventing the equipment that modern cavers use.

Usually he descended into a cave through a pothole. But first he needed to know how deep it was. So he "fished" for the bottom with a cannonball tied to a rope. When the cannonball stopped, Martel measured out that length for a rope ladder, which he tied to heavy stakes pounded into the ground. He always tried to rope off the area to keep spectators away from the hole. (If they came too close, trying to look down on him, they knocked rocks from the edge onto his head.)

Before he went down into the pothole, Martel put on a coverall he invented. Every part of it had pockets to hold his equipment:

- big candles and two boxes of matches wrapped in waterproof cloth
- a holder for a magnesium wire that made brighter light if he needed it

- a plumb line for finding out how deep any shafts were
- a tape measure
- a compass for telling directions
- two thermometers and two barometers for measuring temperatures and air pressure
- a first-aid kit
- pencils and a notebook for writing down his observations
- plenty of chocolate and wine or rum in case he was stranded in the cold

Martel always wore a lifeline to hold him in case he fell off the ladder. Strapped on, somewhere, was the most modern invention—a portable, battery-operated telephone. (His wife was usually at the top, at the receiving end of the telephone. She was afraid of caves and never went down into them.)

Martel used his tape measure to measure the size of a cavern in different directions along the floor. Measuring the height was a bigger problem, which he solved with another invention. He tied a thin string to a paper balloon, hung a sponge underneath it, soaked the sponge with alcohol, and lit it. Hot air from the burning sponge filled the balloon and lifted it to the roof of the cavern, while Martel played out the string. When the balloon reached the cave roof he pulled in the string and measured it.

He kept on inventing—a kind of chair to sit in while being lowered; better ladders; a portable canoe that could be carried in canvas bags. Finally, Martel gave up his law practice entirely and spent all his time exploring caves and lecturing and writing about speleology. He worked to convince scientists that speleology was a science itself, that the study of the world under the earth's surface was an important part of geography.

Martel said that caving was mountaineering in reverse—one simply went down instead of up.

Today, many people enjoy caving as a sport. They visit show caves, but they also enjoy exploring wild caves. Much of the equipment modern cavers use began with Edouard-Alfred Martel. But there have been great advances in technology, so a caver's tools are much better than they were in Martel's time. Modern cavers use:

- a plastic hard hat with a battery-operated or carbide light on it

- tough, warm clothes (cavers get very dirty and caves are cold)
- heavy, nonslip boots (in very fragile areas, cavers change to soft shoes, something like heavy socks)
- a backpack that can hold:

    a first-aid kit

    a flashlight

    candles and waterproof matches

    high-energy candy bars and freeze-dried food to save space

    a compass

    a pad and pencil

    an insulated blanket

- a chest harness and a seat harness (both can be connected to ropes, a steel ladder, and other equipment for moving steadily up and down)

If the cavers are part of an expedition, they also carry other things—inflatable rafts, cameras and lights, walkie-talkies, surveying instruments, laser devices, and computers.

Some cave systems are so huge that they take days or weeks at a time to explore. Then the expedition sets up base camps inside the cave, with supplies, food, and even tents because very big caves sometimes give explorers a lost, spooky feeling. A tent is cozy. It's like home in an unknown place.

If you ever have a chance to do some cave exploring, there are some important rules to remember.

- NEVER go into any cave alone. (That's the most important rule.)
- If you are a beginner, go with an experienced group.
- Always tell someone what cave the group will be in. If it's a big cave system, also tell what part of the cave the group will be in, and the planned time for going in and coming out.
- If the cave is on private property, get permission from the owner.
- Wear warm clothes and gloves, sneakers if the cave is dry, and climbing boots if it's not.

- Be careful climbing up and down. Don't keep going if you are tired. (Tired cavers make mistakes.)
- Wear a hard hat—a bicycle helmet is fine.
- Mark the way in and out, but don't leave marks that can't be erased. Some cavers carry light-reflecting tape. They apply it on formations on the way in and remove it on the way out. Or you might reel out a string from the entrance and follow it back.
- Don't break cave formations. Don't take souvenirs.

If you ever go caving, remember the rules. And have a great adventure!

GLOSSARY

Adaptation: The way any living thing is fitted to the life it leads.
Aquifer: In any place, the permanent zone of underground water.
Archaeology: The science of studying past human life.
Bed: A layer of rock.
Bedding plane: The place where two layers of rock meet.
Bedrock: The bottom layer of solid rock in the earth's crust.
Calcite: The main mineral of limestone.
Carbon dioxide: A gas in the air.
Carbonic acid: The solution of water and carbon dioxide that dissolves limestone to make caves.
Cave: A natural hole in the ground.
Cave pearl: A small, round ball of calcite formed under water.
Caver: A cave explorer.
Cave raft: A flat, floating calcite formation.
Cavern: A cave system.
Cave system: A big cave with many chambers and passages.
Chamber: A very large room in a cave.
Column: A stalactite and stalagmite joined together.

Core: The metallic center of the earth.

Crust: The outer layer of the earth.

Dark zone: A place in a cave where no light enters.

Dead cave: A cave where water no longer builds formations.

Doline: Another name for a sinkhole.

Drapery: A hanging "curtain" formed by seeping water.

Echolocation: The way bats "see" in the dark.

Entrance zone: The entrance area of a cave.

Erosion: The wearing away of the earth's surface by wind, water, or ice.

Flowstone: A cave formation made by flowing water.

Fried eggs: Cave formations in the tops of broken stalagmites.

Geology: The scientific study of the earth and the rocks that make it up.

Geyser: An eruption of steam or heated water from the earth's crust.

Guano: Bat or bird droppings.

Gypsum: A soft form of calcite.

Helictite: Small, curly formations on cave ceilings and walls.

Igneous rock: Rock produced when magma cools and hardens.

Joint: A division through a bed of rock.

Karst: A limestone formation pitted with caves, cracks, potholes, and sinkholes.

Lime: A slightly water-soluble solid obtained from calcite, limestone, or oyster shells.

Limestone: Rock formed from the calcium deposits of ancient sea life.

Live cave: A cave where water still drips and formations continue to grow.

Magma: The flaming-hot rock in the earth's mantle.

Mantle: The layer beneath the earth's crust.

Metamorphic rock: Rock formed under great pressure from either igneous or sedimentary rock.

Passage: A more-or-less horizontal tunnel in a cave.

Photosynthesis: The process by which plants make food for themselves.

Phreatic cave: A cave formed when completely filled with water.

Popcorn (and sea grapes): Small, round formations on cave walls and ceilings.

Pothole: A shaft open to the sky in karst, or inside a cave.

Potholer: A cave explorer.

Sedimentary rock: Rock formed when sediments—shells, soil, minerals—are squeezed together in the crust.

Shaft: The vertical entrance to a cave or a vertical drop inside a cave.

Shelfstone: A flat shelf of stone formed in a cave pool.

Show cave: A cave that has been prepared for visitors with no caving experience.

Sinkhole: A hole on the surface of the earth where the rock has eroded. It can be the entrance to a cave underneath.

Sinter: Any calcite cave formation.

Soda straw: A beginning stalactite.

Speleologist: A scientist who studies caves.

Speleology: The exploration and scientific study of caves.

Spelunker: Another name for a caver.

Stalactite: A calcite formation hanging down from a cave ceiling.

Stalagmite: A formation reaching up from a cave floor, built by calcite dripping from the stalactite above it.

Tectonic plate: A section of the earth's crust.

Totem pole: A thin stalagmite.

Troglobite: An animal living only in the dark zone of a cave.

Troglophile: An animal living in the twilight zone of a cave. Most troglophiles sleep during the day and leave the cave at night for food.

Trogloxene. An animal that lives in and out of the entrance zone of a cave.

Twilight zone: The dim-light area of a cave.

Vadose cave: A cave formed by running water with air above it.

Water table: The surface of the aquifer.

Wild cave: An unexplored or partly unexplored cave.

INDEX

(Page numbers in *italic* refer to illustrations.)